THIS CANDLEWICK BOOK BELONGS TO:

Aiden Sullivan

Love,

Nana + Pappy 2007

For Susan

First U.S. paperback edition 2006

Library of Congress Cataloging-in-Publication Data is available.

Library of Congress Catalog Card Number 98-014051

ISBN-13: 978-0-7636-0710-4 (hardcover)
ISBN-10: 0-7636-0710-X (hardcover)
ISBN-13: 978-0-7636-3217-5 (paperback)
ISBN-10: 0-7636-3217-1 (paperback)

2 4 6 8 10 9 7 5 3 1

Printed in China

This book was typeset in Kabel Book Alt.
The illustrations were done in watercolor and ink.

Candlewick Press
2067 Massachusetts Avenue
Cambridge, Massachusetts 02140

visit us at www.candlewick.com

Bunny My Honey

Anita Jeram

CANDLEWICK PRESS

CAMBRIDGE, MASSACHUSETTS

Mommy Rabbit had a baby.
His name was Bunny.
He looked just like his mommy,
only smaller.

He had long ears, a twitchy nose,
and great big feet.
"Bunny, my Honey,"
Mommy Rabbit liked to call him.

Mommy Rabbit showed Bunny how to
do special rabbity things,

like running and hopping,

digging and twitching his nose,

and thumping his great big feet.

Sometimes Bunny played with his best friends,
Little Duckling and Miss Mouse.
They played quack-quacky games,
squeaky games, and thump-thump-thumpy
games.

They sang, *We're the little Honeys.*
A little Honey is sweet.
Quack quack, squeak squeak,
Thump your great big feet!

If a game ever ended in tears,
as games sometimes do,
Mommy Rabbit made it better.

"Don't cry, my little Honeys,"
Mommy Rabbit said. "I'm right here."

But one day Bunny got lost.

Oh, how could such a bad thing happen?

Perhaps it was a game that went wrong.

Perhaps Bunny ran too far on his own.

But there he was,
just one lost Bunny.

The more Bunny looked for
his friends and his mommy
the more lost
and the more lost
and the more lost
he became.

Bunny started to cry.
"Mommy, Mommy,
I want my mommy!
Mommy, Mommy,
I want my mommy!"

"Bunny, my Honey!"

What was that?

"Bunny, my Honey!

Bunny, my Honey!"

"Bunny, my Honey!"

Mommy Rabbit picked
Bunny up and cuddled him.
She stroked his long ears.
She put her twitchy nose
on his twitchy nose.
She kissed his great big feet.
Bunny's ears and nose
and feet felt warm all over.

"I love you, Mommy,"
Bunny whispered.
"I love you, Bunny, my Honey,"
Bunny's mommy
whispered back,
"and I love my other
little Honeys, too."

On the way home, Bunny and
Miss Mouse and Little Duckling
sang their song.

We're the little Honeys.
A little Honey is sweet.
Quack quack, squeak squeak,
Thump your great big feet!

And Bunny was a
happy rabbit.

Anita Jeram is the critically acclaimed illustrator of numerous children's books, including the phenomenal bestseller *Guess How Much I Love You*™ by Sam McBratney, and the author and illustrator of several other books for children.

Of *Bunny, My Honey*, she says, "Small children don't realize how dependent they are on their parents until they lose contact with them. It doesn't matter if they're only one aisle over in the supermarket—it feels like a hundred miles away. The world seems a much bigger and scarier place when you're disconnected from the ones who love you." Anita Jeram lives in Northern Ireland with her paleontologist husband and their three children.